D0625719

ADVENTURES of the
STEAMPUNK PiRATES

Rise of the Slippery Sea Monster

Essex County Council

3013021138973 8

For my crew of scurvy scallywags:
Lisa, Herbie & Autumn – GPJ

To David. Cheers for all the years x – FAD

STRIPES PUBLISHING
An imprint of Little Tiger Press
1 The Coda Centre, 189 Munster Road,
London SW6 6AW

A paperback original
First published in Great Britain in 2016

Text copyright © Gareth P. Jones, 2016
Illustrations copyright © Artful Doodlers, 2016
Cover typeface courtesy of www.shutterstock.com

ISBN: 978-1-84715-664-8

The rights of Gareth P. Jones and Artful Doodlers to
be identified as the author and illustrator of this work
respectively has been asserted by them in accordance
with the Copyright, Designs and Patents Act, 1988.

All rights reserved.

This book is sold subject to the condition that it shall not,
by way of trade or otherwise, be lent, resold, hired out, or
otherwise circulated without the publisher's prior consent
in any form of binding or cover other than that in which it
is published and without a similar condition, including this
condition, being imposed upon the subsequent purchaser.

A CIP catalogue record for this book is available
from the British Library.

Printed and bound in the UK.

10 9 8 7 6 5 4 3 2 1

ADVENTURES of the
Steampunk
PiRates

Rise of the Slippery Sea Monster

Gareth P. Jones

Stripes

WANTED

DEAD OR ALIVE!
(or smashed into little bits and delivered in boxes)

The crew of the *Leaky Battery* the STEAMPUNK PIRATES for piracy, looting and treason.

Sixteen scurrilous scallywags in total,
including their four officers:

CAPTAIN CLOCKHEART
Hot-headed leader of
the Steampunk Pirates.
He is unpredictable and
dangerous on account of
a loose valve sending too
much steam to his head.

FIRST MATE MAINSPRING
Operated by clockwork,
he is at his most devious
when overly wound up.

QUARTERMASTER LEXI
Fitted with a catalogue
of information, he is
the cleverest (if not the
bravest) of the bunch.

MR GADGE
His various arm attachments
include all kinds of devilish
weaponry and fighting
equipment.

A REWARD OF
FOUR THOUSAND POUNDS
is offered for anyone who captures this
crew of loathsome looters and returns
them to their rightful owner,
the King of England.

We are the Steampunk Pirates,
We're tireless, true and tough,
We sail across the ocean,
Through waters, calm or rough,
We'll plunder, pinch and pillage,
Then sail off with your stuff,
We'll take it all,
Big or small,
But it's never quite enough,
(Enough!)
It's never quite enough!

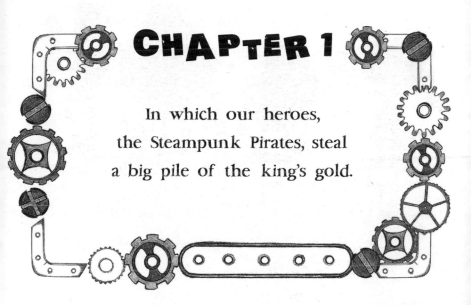

CHAPTER 1

In which our heroes,
the Steampunk Pirates, steal
a big pile of the king's gold.

It had been another successful raid for the
Steampunk Pirates. They had boarded the
transporter ship and forced the sailors to their
knees with their hands behind their heads.

Gadge used the bayonet attachment on
his left arm to push the ship's commander to
the tip of an extremely wobbly plank.

First Mate Mainspring emerged from the hold with a large wooden chest.

"What cargo have we here then?" asked Captain Clockheart.

"**Click**, it's heavy enough. **Tick**, whatever it is." The clockwork first mate dropped the chest.

"Put that chest back, you copper-bottomed cads," cried the ship's commander.

"Copper bottomed? These backsides be made of iron. Ain't that so, Lexi?" Captain Clockheart slapped Quartermaster Lexi's behind.

"We are indeed made from iron, yes," said Lexi primly. "And please don't do that, Captain."

"I don't care what you're made of, you metal menaces! I order you to return that chest," yelled the commander.

"Following orders ain't exactly one of our strong points, laddie." Gadge stamped his foot on the plank. The other pirates howled with laughter as the commander tried to keep his balance.

Captain Clockheart prised the chest open with his cutlass. "Ah, pump my pistons! A chest full of golden delights!"

"This should help considerably in our quest to replace our rusting parts," said Lexi.

"That gold does not belong to you," protested the commander.

"**Click**, it does now," said First Mate Mainspring. "**Tick**, Mr Pumps, Loose-screw, Tin-pot Paddy and Rust-knuckles. **Tock**, load this gold on to the *Leaky Battery*."

Quartermaster Lexi lifted out one of the gold bars to examine it. "Mmm, yes. Eighteen carat." He sniffed it. "Freshly mined from the west coast of America."

"You can get all that from the smell, Lexi?" asked Pendle, the cabin boy.[1]

---

1 If you are a newcomer to this most excellent series, you should know that Pendle the cabin boy is, in fact, a girl. Also, where on earth have you been?

"No, the details are printed on each bar," admitted Lexi. "There's a royal stamp, too."

"Royal gold! Royal gold!" Twitter, the mechanical parrot, squawked.

"Precisely," said the commander. "This gold belongs to the King of England."

"So do we according to our 'Wanted' poster. We be worth four thousand pounds now." Captain Clockheart beat his chest proudly, making the hand on the clock in the centre of his chest spin twice as fast. "It warms the lumps of coal in me belly to feel wanted, so it does. Now, back to our ship, Steampunk Pirates! We have some celebrating to do."

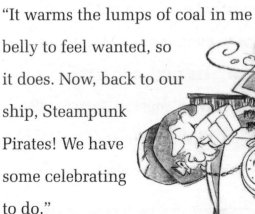

"Celebrating?" exclaimed the commander. "How can machines celebrate?"

"The same way as you do," said Captain Clockheart. "With songs, laughter, food and liquid."

"What do you eat and drink?" the commander asked.

"We consume the four main food groups, of course," said Lexi. "Coal, wood, oil and water."

"Talking of water…" Gadge fired a grappling hook at a high crossbeam on the *Leaky Battery* and swung back to the ship, knocking the commander into the ocean with a huge SPLASH! The rest of the pirates gave a rousing HURRAH!

"You scrap-metal scalliwags," spluttered the commander, when he bobbed up to the

surface. "You dare steal from the King of England? This is treason. Treason, I say!"

"Treason..." Lexi's word-wheel spun round until it reached the definition of the word. "The betrayal of one's country."

"You call it treason, we call it freedom." Captain Clockheart picked up a large silver tankard. "Now, lads, it's time to fill our hold with gold, our sails with wind and our cups with oil. All hail the Steampunk Pirates!"

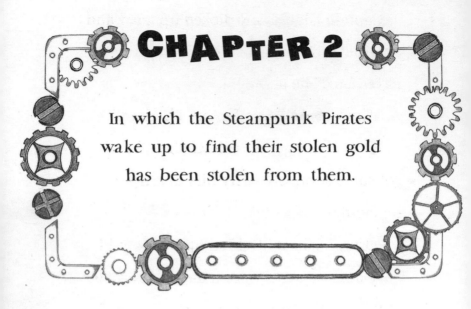

CHAPTER 2

In which the Steampunk Pirates
wake up to find their stolen gold
has been stolen from them.

Propelled by its full sails and its pumping
steam engine, the *Leaky Battery* cut through
the clear blue ocean at high speed. The
crew sang and laughed as they took the gold
down to the hold, while Lexi counted each
bar and jotted down the total on a piece
of parchment.

Captain Clockheart picked up a bar and admired it. "How much do you reckon we have then?" he asked.

"Almost a quarter of a ton, I believe."

"Och, that's good," said Gadge. "I've got some seriously rusty bits that need replacing."

"Once it's been divided up, we should have at least enough for a new hand each," replied Lexi. "Maybe even a whole arm."

First Mate Mainspring lowered his voice. "**Click**, why should we split it evenly? **Tick**, we're the officers. **Tock**, we're more important than the crew."

"Now, Mainspring, you know that's not how we do things on this ship," said Captain Clockheart. "We officers may have more complex workings, but every pirate on this ship was created equal. From Old Tinder down in the kitchen to Blower up in the crow's nest, everyone has earned his fair share of that loot, whether they're clockwork, steam-powered or flesh and bone."

"All equal!" squawked Twitter, flying around their heads. "All equal!"

"**Click**, equal? **Tick**, my clockwork innards make me superior to you coal-munching machines. **Tock**, especially you, you feather-brained bird."

Twitter swooped to avoid being hit by Mainspring's cutlass.

Captain Clockheart laughed and took a swig from the tankard Pendle handed him. "Eurgh." He spat out the contents. "Pendle, there are bits in this oil."

"Sorry. I'll get it filtered," said Pendle.

"Good lad. Also, that kindling you brought me for breakfast was damp."

"Sorry, Captain."

"Damp kindling makes me awful gassy." He demonstrated with a long burp and a jet of steam came from his mouth.

"It won't happen again, Captain."

Captain Clockheart patted Pendle on the head and said, "Now, let's get the coal burning, the wood chipping and the night oil bubbling... This evening we shall party like it's 1899."

"**Click**, these celebrations," said Mainspring. "**Tick**, are a total waste of time.

Tock, when I'm captain—"

"Ah, Mainspring." Captain Clockheart placed an arm around his first mate's shoulder. "Has anyone ever told you that you're too uptight? You want to unwind a little." He whacked the key on Mainspring's back, making it spin round.

"**Click**, get your hands off me," muttered Mainspring. "**Tick**, if I was captain, **tock**, I'd make sure officers got what they deserved."

"Yes, but you're not the captain, are you?" Captain Clockheart gripped Mainspring's arms.

"That would be me."

Mainspring shook himself free. "**Click**, I hope you drink so much oil. **Tick**, that you slide off the ship. **Tock**, and sink like a lead weight."

"Ah, be off with you, you prickly old pocket watch!" Captain Clockheart replied. "Go and sulk down below if you're going to be a party pooper. Now, how about a song to kick off this celebration?"

Gadge threw back his head and sang at the top of his voice:

Chop, chop, chop the wood,
To keep your fires burning,
Drink, drink, drink the oil,
Make sure your engine's turning,
Chomp, chomp, chomp the coal,
Until the day be dawning,
Pour, pour, pour the oil,
Then poor me in the morning!

The party went on late and Pendle spent the whole night refilling tankards of oil, collecting piles of wood and sweeping up ash, until finally she fell asleep in the middle of a large coil of rope.

When she awoke, she rubbed her bleary eyes, got up and tucked her hair back into her cap. Washer Williams and Blind Bob Bolt were the only pirates still awake. They were singing a shanty, although neither of them could remember the words:

There was a young someone,
Who sailed somewhere far,
He did something funny,
Tra-la-la-la,
He somethinged and somethinged,
Do-dar-diddy-door,
Then something happened,
Now he'll something no more!

Pendle headed below deck to find a mop. There were pirates all over the place, snoring, snuffling and snorting in their sleep.

Twitter landed on Pendle's shoulder. "Lazy lot!" he squawked. "Lazy lot!"

"Leave them," said Pendle. "They deserve to let off steam after such a successful raid."

Pendle noticed that the door to the cabin where the treasure had been stored was knocking against its frame. She grabbed the handle to shut it and felt a cold breeze. Peering in, she saw that a perfectly circular hole had been cut in the side of the ship. The sun was shining through it and water was splashing in.

"Where's the treasure?" gasped Pendle.

"Gold has gone!" squawked Twitter. "Gold has gone!"

"But how? What's happened?"

"Foul play! Foul play!" replied Twitter.

"I'd better tell the captain at once," said Pendle. "Twitter, wake everyone up. NOW!"

Twitter flew out through the hole in the side of the ship and up to the deck, swooping and looping as he announced the news at the top of his voice.

"Wake up! Wake up! We've been robbed! We've been robbed!"

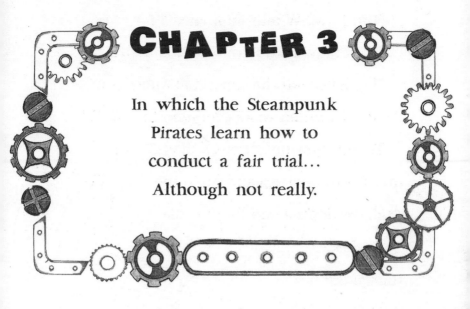

CHAPTER 3

In which the Steampunk
Pirates learn how to
conduct a fair trial...
Although not really.

Captain Clockheart was the first to join
Pendle in the hold but, with Twitter
spreading the news, a number of bleary-eyed
pirates were soon gathered in the doorway.

"Well, shiver me tin chin and polish me
ten toes." Captain Clockheart placed a hand
on the edge of the hole in the ship's side.

He wiped the sea spray from his face. "What's happened here then?"

"I can't understand it," said Pendle.

"**Click**, make way. **Tick**, officers coming through. **Tock**, out of the way, you useless lot of deck scrubbers." Mainspring, Lexi and Gadge entered the cabin.

Gadge flicked out his magnifying-glass attachment to examine the hole. "Looks like something has cut straight through," he said.

"Perhaps Blower saw something," said Lexi. "He was on lookout all night."

"I'll ask him," said Pendle, and she raced off.

"**Click**, this is your fault, Clockheart," said Mainspring. "**Tick**, for letting your guard down. **Tock**, and spending all night celebrating."

"A celebration that you did not attend." Captain Clockheart turned to face the clockwork pirate. "Which puts you under suspicion, so I say."

"**Click**, me? **Tick**, how dare you? **Tock**, it wasn't me."

"Mainspring, main suspect!" squawked Twitter. "Mainspring, main suspect!"

"He did admit to being fed up of sharing the loot," added Gadge.

"Greedy schemer!" added Twitter. "Greedy schemer!"

Pendle rushed back into the cabin and caught her breath. "Blower says that no ship came near all night."

"So he didn't see what happened?" asked Lexi.

"No, but you can't see this part of the ship from the crow's nest because of the sails."

"Ha, then it must have been one of us." The captain's clock hand span faster and steam shot out of his ears. "Mainspring, you've got some explaining to do."

"**Click**, you can't just accuse me. **Tick**, you need evidence. **Tock**, and you don't have any."

"Evidence…" Lexi's word-wheel turned and clicked into place. "Proof that the accused committed the crime."

"Mainspring is right, Captain," said Pendle.

"If you really think he is behind this, you need to conduct a fair trial."

"A fair trial…" said Lexi. "A formal hearing in front of a jury."

"Yes," said Pendle. "Then Mainspring can defend himself properly. The crew can act as jury."

"What do you say, lads? Shall we have ourselves a fair trial to convict Mainspring?" Captain Clockheart asked.

The crew cheered and Twitter squawked, "Fair trial! Fair trial! Convict Mainspring! Convict Mainspring!"

Soon the entire crew had gathered up top and Captain Clockheart stood on the poop deck looking down at them.

When Quartermaster Lexi led First Mate Mainspring up to his position beside the captain, the crew jeered "Thief!", "Convict!" and "Gold stealer!".

"**Click**, I'm innocent," protested Mainspring.

"'I'm innocent' protests guilty first mate!" cried Twitter.

"**Tick**, hush your beak, you stupid parrot!" Mainspring tried to swat the bird. "**Tock**, before I cut you down."

"Guilty first mate attacks beloved ship's bird!" squawked Twitter.

"Stop it, Twitter," pleaded Pendle. "This is supposed to be a fair trial."

"A fair trial about what?" asked Loose-screw, who had only just woken up. "What's going on?"

"This is a trial to find out whether

Mainspring took the treasure," said Pendle.

"Did he just say Mainspring took the treasure?" Blind Bob Bolt asked loudly. "It's an outrage."

"No, no, no," said Pendle. "This is a hearing."

"Yes, I am," said Blind Bob Bolt.

"You are what?" said Loose-screw.

"Hard of hearing. My ears are all clogged up with oil and seaweed."

"**Click**, this isn't a trial about your ears," said Mainspring. "**Tick**, can we get on with it, please? **Tock**, we need to repair that hole in the ship!"

Captain Clockheart cleared his throat and released a jet of steam. "First Mate Mainspring," he cried. "Ever since we escaped from the king's palace and set sail in search of a better life, you have tried to take control of this ship. Is that not so?"

"**Click**, aye, but only because I knew I could do a better job of—"

Captain Clockheart cut him off. "And is it not also true that yesterday you moaned about having to share our latest haul?"

"**Tick**, aye, but—"

"And because you were fed up of sharing, did you not decide to steal the gold?" Captain Clockheart brought his fist down.

"**Tock**, no! Of course not—"

"Admit it. You took the gold and now you must be punished. All hail the Steampunk Pirates!" Captain Clockheart raised his fist and the crew cheered. "I rest my case."

"Now Mainspring must defend himself," said Pendle.

Mainspring looked at the crew with weary eyes. "**Click**, I didn't take the treasure. How could I have done? **Tick**, where would I put it? I'm on the same ship as you. **Tock**, now, can we please get back to finding out who really did take it?"

"What's he saying?" asked Blind Bob Bolt.

"He asked us where he put the gold," said Loose-screw.

"How would we know? He's the one who took it," said Mr Pumps.

"To be sure, he did," said Tin-pot Paddy. "The captain just told us that. Wasn't he listening?"

"Maybe he's got oil in his ears, too," said Blind Bob Bolt.

"Mainspring, can't you defend yourself better than that?" asked Pendle. "What about saying where you were at the time of the theft? Or how you'd never steal from your shipmates? Anything. Please."

"**Click**, why should I? **Tick**, I didn't do it. **Tock**, there's nothing else to say." Mainspring glared at the other pirates defiantly, his arms folded.

"So what happens now?" asked Lexi.

"The crew must decide," said Pendle. "Is Mainspring guilty or—"

The rest of the sentence was cut off by the crew's jeers.

"Aye!"

"Guilty."

"Gold thief! Gold thief!"

"You see?" said Captain Clockheart. "Now, Mr Mainspring, return the treasure."

Mainspring sighed. "**Click**, I can't return it. **Tick**, I didn't take it. **Tock**, can't you get that into your thick tin head?"

"We'll see who's head is thick," said Captain Clockheart. "It's punishment time."

"Captain, this is a bad idea," said Pendle.

"No. Mainspring must be punished!" Captain Clockheart replied. "Not long ago we passed a small desert island. We'll leave him there to think about what he's done."

"**Click**, this is unfair. **Tick**, I'm innocent…"

But the crew didn't care about Mainspring's protests. The trial had been conducted and he had been convicted. As far as they were concerned, First Mate Mainspring had taken the gold and now he would pay for his crime.

The author apologizes for this interruption, but he wonders if some readers might like to know what has happened to the Iron Duke and Admiral Fussington.

The two high-ranking military men stood behind a large bush in the middle of Hyde Park in London. In front of them was a small dog.

The Iron Duke took aim with his pistol. "You no-good snivelling scoundrel," he said. "You thought you could get away from us!

Well, you didn't reckon on the superior intellect of the Iron Duke. Now, prepare to pay for your actions."

"Er, Duke," whispered Admiral Fussington nervously. "We're not actually supposed to shoot His Majesty's pets."

The Iron Duke kept his gun aimed at the corgi. "Why ever not?" he said.

"We're only supposed to be cleaning up after their ... er, their deposits."

The Iron Duke lowered his weapon reluctantly and the dog trotted away.

"Now, shall I do the scooping, or do you want to?" Admiral Fussington held up a small trowel and a dustpan.

"This is so embarrassing," said the Iron Duke. "And it's all your fault, Fussington."

"I'm not sure that's entirely fair," protested the admiral. "We are both responsible for the Steampunk Pirates escaping." He bent down and scooped up the dog mess.

"It takes a wise man to devise a brilliant plan, but any old fool to muck it up," the duke replied. "Thanks to your repeated incompetence, we are cleaning up after these royal rodents, while those tin-can terrors roam free."

Admiral Fussington stood up straight. "I don't think they are rodents, technically speaking." He held up the dustpan. "Do you have any more of those little bags?"

"Admiral Fussington, you beef-headed buffoon, the Iron Duke is a name that strikes fear into a thousand hearts! I am a master of the ocean! No, I do not have any more poo bags."

"Duke! Admiral!" yelled the king from the other side of the bush. "I'm afraid that Mr Pitt the Younger has a rather upset tummy. I blame the prunes he had for breakfast. Anyhow, there's more scooping needed."

"He'll have more than an upset tummy once I'm through with the miserable mutt," snarled the Iron Duke.

"What was that?" called the king.

"Did you say something, Duke?"

"We'll be right there," said Admiral Fussington.

"Excellent," said the king. "Remember, if you do a good job, I may allow you to return to my navy one day."

"But, Your Majesty—" said the Iron Duke.

"Silence." The king cut him off. "As it is, I shall shortly be setting sail to the Americas without you."

"But that is a dangerous route. You'll be sailing through pirate waters," said Admiral Fussington. "Who will protect you?"

"I'm taking Corporal Thudchump."

"Thudchump?" barked the duke. "But the man's an idiot."

"In my experience, it takes one to know one," the king replied.

"But, Your Majesty," said the Iron Duke. "I am begging you—"

The king interrupted him. "The only begging I want to see is from my precious pooches. Now, come forth and pick up this poo, or I shall keep you scooping poop until you are too old to stoop."

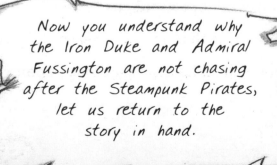

Now you understand why the Iron Duke and Admiral Fussington are not chasing after the Steampunk Pirates, let us return to the story in hand.

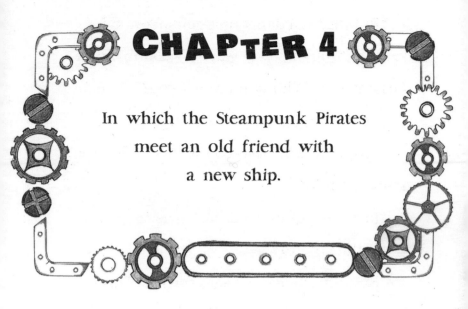

CHAPTER 4

In which the Steampunk Pirates
meet an old friend with
a new ship.

"Yo ho, down below!" cried Blower from the crow's nest, as they sailed away from the desert island where they had left Mainspring. "Pirate ship ahoy and it's sailing straight towards us."

"You hear that, my salty seacogs?" yelled Captain Clockheart. "Load the cannons, but

hold your fire. We'll give them no excuse to attack … but we'll be ready if they do."

Gadge pulled out his extendable telescopic eye to get a better look.

"What can you see, Mr Gadge?" asked the captain.

"Looks like a pretty standard ragbag mix of scallywags," he said. "Hold on. Och, now there's a familiar face and a few familiar tentacles, too… It's Inkybeard!"

"Squid head's back!" squawked Twitter. "Squid head's back!"

"The Dread Captain Inkybeard." Lexi's word-wheel span and clicked. "The infamous pirate captain with—"

"A squid called Nancy on his head. Yes, yes, we know," interrupted Captain Clockheart.[2] However, as the nameless ship

2 Lexi was actually about to say: "The Dread Captain Inkybeard, the infamous pirate captain with a reputation for sinking his own ships at the first sign of mutiny."

drew alongside the *Leaky Battery*, it became apparent that the creature resting on top of Captain Inkybeard's black hair was not a squid, but an octopus.

"New friend, Inkybeard?" said Captain Clockheart.

"Yes, this is Nell, me new wife," replied the pirate.

"What happened to Nancy?" asked Pendle.

The octopus squeezed the tentacle that was wrapped around Inkybeard's neck, cutting off his windpipe. She allowed him to struggle for a moment then released her grip.

Inkybeard took a deep breath. "Ouch. I'll ask you not to mention that name. Nell gets ever so jealous, so she does. She's a little possessive."

"So are we," added one of Inkybeard's pirates, with black teeth and a striped bandana. "And we want our treasure back."

Inkybeard waved his cutlass at the pirate. "Quiet. As captain, Inkybeard will do the asking. Now, Clockheart, what have you done with my treasure?"

"What treasure?" said Captain Clockheart.

"Captain, look." Pendle pointed to a perfectly round hole in the side of Inkybeard's ship. A few planks of wood had been nailed over it, but it looked like the job had been done in a hurry.

"Yes, we woke up this morning to find

someone had pilfered our haul," said Inkybeard. "And we know it was you what took it! Yours is the only ship for miles around."

"We know the rules, laddie," said Gadge. "Pirates don't steal from fellow pirates."

"And we know that there is no such thing as a fellow pirate," said Inkybeard. "Eh, Nancy?" A tentacle squeezed his shoulder. "Ow! Nell, I meant Nell."

"We didn't take your stinking treasure," said Captain Clockheart.

"That's right," said Pendle. "The same thing happened to us."

"Enough excuses!" said Inkybeard. "Now, we're going to board your ship and retrieve our stolen loot, ain't we, lads?"

Inkybeard's brutish pirates picked

up muskets, pistols and cutlasses. They lowered a boarding plank and a heavily tattooed pirate stepped on to it.

"If it's a fight you be wanting, you've come to the right place." Captain Clockheart jabbed his cutlass towards the pirate, who toppled into the ocean. "My marvellous metal marauders, defend our ship!"

The Steampunk Pirates grabbed their weapons and prepared to fight, but just then a voice from above cried, "Wait!"

Both crews looked up to see a young man with wavy brown hair, smart stripy trousers and a fashionable shirt.

Once he had everyone's attention, the boy leaped from his position halfway up the main mast on Inkybeard's ship, with his arms outstretched. He fell for a moment,

then grabbed a rope and swung over to
the jib. He used the sail to swing on to a
crossbeam, spun round it twice, then soared
into the air before landing gracefully on the
deck beside Inkybeard. Everyone watched
open-mouthed.

"Ah, Kidd, my boy," said Inkybeard, patting him on the back affectionately. "We're about to wreak our revenge on this shipload of steam-heads and take back our treasure."

"With all due respect, Dread Captain Inkybeard, sir, and apologies for speaking out of turn," said the boy. "I realize I am only an ever-so-humble cabin boy, but I do not think these iron gentlemen are to blame for our missing treasure."

"Who is this wordy youngster, Inkybeard?" asked Captain Clockheart.

"This be our cabin boy," said Inkybeard.

Kidd walked along the ship's plank, bounced a couple of times then performed a triple somersault in the air and landed on the *Leaky Battery*.

"The name's Kidd. You've probably heard of me."

"No," said Pendle.

"Really? They say I'm the best pirate's cabin boy in the ocean. I've served on more pirate ships than you have barnacles on your keel. The *Black Skull*, the *Flying Pig*, the *Cutty Razor*, the *Pimply Bottom*... I've sailed on them all."

"Aye, Kidd, but where's our treasure if it's not on their ship?" said Inkybeard.

"Oh yes, the treasure," said Kidd. "I was considering this mysterious theft when I remembered a leaflet I was recently handed in Barbary Bay." He pulled out a rolled-up parchment from his back pocket.

Captain Clockheart snatched it then handed it to Lexi to read out.

BEWARE YE, PIRATES ALL . . .
THE SLIPPERY SEA MONSTER!

Sailors beware, if you sail much farther,
Than Blood Orange Island or Rotten Apple Harbour.
A thing lives down there, deeper than deep,
This slippery monster strikes while you sleep.

They say that this monster comes up from its lair,
To cut holes in ships and take what is there.
Only pirate ships are this monster's prey,
The slippery sea monster slips clean away.

It leaves these ships floating,
(Although somewhat lighter,)
All pirates curse this gold-robbing blighter.
A trail of bubbles reveal where it's been,
But the slippery monster has never been seen.

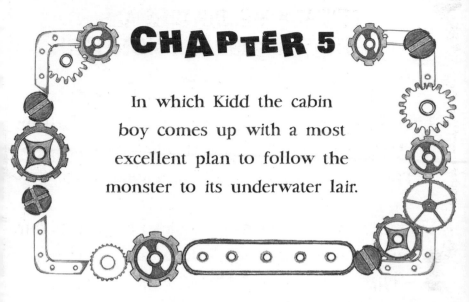

CHAPTER 5

In which Kidd the cabin
boy comes up with a most
excellent plan to follow the
monster to its underwater lair.

When Lexi had finished reading the poem,
he looked up and said, "It does fit with what
happened to us."

"Hold on," said Gadge. "If it was this
monster that took our treasure then
Mainspring was wrongly convicted."

The Steampunk Pirates gasped in

disbelief, but Pendle sighed. "Of course he was," she said. "That trial was about as fair as Inkybeard's black beard, but a sea monster that steals gold? It's ridiculous. And why would it cut such round holes?"

"Sea monster..." Lexi's word-wheel clicked into action. "A mythological creature said to dwell in the ocean, often the source of fear and superstition among sailors."

Captain Clockheart stroked his spring beard thoughtfully. "I say we hunt down this creature and give him a taste of the sharp end of our cutlasses."

Kidd jumped up and grabbed a boom, then hoisted himself up on to it. "Fellow pirates, I have a cunning scheme to suggest."

He scampered up the rigging of the *Leaky Battery* and took hold of a rope hanging from

the crow's nest.
Then he swung
round the mast and
landed with one foot on
each ship. Once again,
his acrobatic display drew
astonished "Oohs" and "Ahhs"
from pirates on both ships.

"We know that this slippery sea monster
hunts in these waters," said Kidd. "So we'll
need bait to coax it out."

"Don't worry, Nell. He don't mean you."
Inkybeard threw a tankard of water over
the octopus then turned back to Kidd.
"You don't mean her, do you?"

"He means treasure," said Pendle.

"Ain't both ships cleared out of treasure?"
asked Captain Clockheart.

"Yes," said Kidd, "but if Inkybeard loots another merchant ship then takes his ill-gotten booty to Rotten Apple Harbour, we'll have the perfect thing to lure this monster out."

"Looting and luring is all very well, so long as it's followed by a bit of blasting and sinking," said Captain Clockheart.

"No," said Kidd. "We must *allow* the monster to steal the treasure."

"What?" said Inkybeard. "Rob us a second time. Why?"

"Because we need to locate the monster's lair and retrieve our gold. The *Leaky Battery* will be waiting nearby to watch the monster get the treasure. According to that rhyme, it'll leave a trail of bubbles, which will lead us all the way back to its lair."

"But what if the rhyme isn't accurate?

And what if—" Lexi was cut off by a sharp bash to the head from Captain Clockheart that instantly shut him down.

"Now is no time for what ifs," Captain Clockheart said. "This monster took our treasure. Now we're going to take it back. This plan be to my liking, Master Kidd."

"Lexi is right. This is a bad idea," said Pendle.

"Bad idea! Bad idea!" repeated Twitter.

"Ah, but you said that about leaving Mainspring on an island," said Captain Clockheart dismissively.

"Yes, and I was right about that, too! He's innocent!" protested Pendle. "We should be getting our first mate back, rather than working with this kid who we don't even know."

"Now, Pendle lad, I know you're jealous of this cabin boy…"

"Pendle's jealous!" squawked Twitter. "Pendle's jealous!"

"No, I'm not," Pendle replied.

"There's no need to be jealous." Kidd jumped down between the ships, grabbed the end of the *Leaky Battery*'s plank and flipped himself back up again. He landed next to Pendle. "Like yourself, I am just an ever-so-humble cabin boy."

"Ha, I like the cut of Master Kidd's jib," said Captain Clockheart.

"This is all very well," said Inkybeard, "but if we end up with a fresh hole in our hull while you bunch of bashed-up buccaneers go after the monster, what's to stop you running off with all the treasure?"

"My word," said Captain Clockheart, offering his hand.

"And our honour," added Gadge.

"Inkybeard don't hold much weight in the words and honour of pirates," said Inkybeard. "We wants a guarantee you'll come back."

"What kind of guarantee?" asked Gadge.

"I know… We'll take your cabin boy," replied Inkybeard. "We knows how valuable Pendle is to you. He mends your broken bits, oils your joints and maintains that engine of yours. We'll keep him till you return with our half of the treasure."

"All right," said Captain Clockheart. "So long as we get our lad back."

"And since there is no need for two cabin boys on one ship," said Kidd. "I will sail

with the Steampunk Pirates. I'd be honoured to add the *Leaky Battery* to the list of great pirate ships upon which I have served."

"Then we have a deal," said Captain Clockheart.

"But, Captain—" began Pendle.

"Don't worry, lad, it won't be for long," Captain Clockheart said.

Kidd winked at Pendle. "Please allow me to show you around your new ship. Don't worry, this crew may look like a band of ruthless rogues, but they serve their purpose. I wouldn't get on the wrong side of them though, if I were you."

Pendle looked into Kidd's sparkling brown eyes. "I'll find my own way," she said. "Besides, I'll be back on my own ship soon enough."

There was a whirring sound as Lexi came back to life. "I say, what's going on?"

"We're swapping cabin boys then going after the monster to get back our treasure," said Gadge.

"Oh dear," said Lexi. "Is that entirely wise?"

"Piracy ain't about wisdom. It's about boldness, braveness and bashing people on the head," said Captain Clockheart. "Now, let's go monster hunting."

The author apologizes for this second interruption, but he wonders if you might be interested in catching up with First Mate Mainspring as he gets into an argument with a tree.

Marooned on a tiny desert island with only a palm tree for company, Mainspring was alone for the first time in his life. To help cope with this new experience, he had taken to talking to the island's only other occupant – the tree.

"**Click**, now, Mr Tree," he said. "**Tick**, we

need to work out how to turn my key. **Tock**, to prevent me from winding down."

Mr Tree didn't respond, but Mainspring nodded as though he was listening intently.

"**Click**, what's that you say? I could ask a passing bird? **Tick**, there are two problems with that, Mr Tree. **Tock**, firstly, I haven't seen a passing bird. Secondly, birds cannot speak."

Again, Mainspring paid close attention to the tree's silent reply.

"**Click**, what's that, you can't speak either? **Tick**, why, Mr Tree, you are too modest. You are a most gifted speaker. **Tock**, now, be a good fellow and wind me up, would you?"

Mainspring turned around and tried to wedge his key into the trunk. The tree shook and a coconut fell on his head.

DONK!

"**Click**, now, Mr Tree," said Mainspring. "**Tick**, there's no need for that. **Tock**, let's try again."

He made a second attempt to wedge his key in, but a second coconut landed on his head.

DONK!

"**Click**, if that's your attitude –" Mainspring wagged his finger furiously at the tree – "**Tick**, you and I are not going to get on. **Tock**, not at all." He grabbed the trunk and shook it violently.

DONK! DONK! DONK!

Three more coconuts dropped down. Mainspring's head was becoming increasingly dented. "**Click**, you think you're so great with your big leaves. **Tick**, well, I've got something to tell you. **Tock**, you're just a stupid old palm tree on a stupid old island."

Mainspring stormed off, but the island was so small that it wasn't long before he was back in his original spot.

"**Click**, I think it's time for a change around here. **Tick**, I've been talking to the sand and the rock, and we've decided that you've been ruling this island too long, Mr Tree. **Tock**, this be mutiny. Mutiny, I say! I'm in charge now. You hear me?"

First Mate Mainspring drove his cutlass into the tree bark. "Ha!" he cried victoriously.

The tree made no response.

Mainspring tried to retrieve his blade, but it was stuck. "If that's how you want to play it…" Mainspring placed a foot on the trunk and yanked. He pulled with all his weight and finally the cutlass came free. The tree rocked back, causing the final coconut to drop on his head, landing with a DONK!

The author apologizes for the extreme silliness of this interruption and suggests you get back to the story in hand.

CHAPTER 6

In which Kidd the
cabin boy makes a
good impression on the
Steampunk Pirates.

The *Leaky Battery* dropped anchor just
along the coast from Rotten Apple Harbour
and waited for Inkybeard's ship to arrive.
With the sails rolled up and the engine
turned off, the Steampunk Pirates occupied
themselves in other ways. Some cleaned the
ship or rowed to shore to collect fresh wood.

Up in the crow's nest, Blower played a tin whistle. Gadge sat on the port side of the ship, whittling a piece of wood with a sharp knife attachment.

Kidd proved to be extremely popular with the crew. When he wasn't swinging from rope to rope in spectacular displays of acrobatics, he was making himself useful. He oiled joints that needed oiling, hammered out dents and listened to the pirates' grumbles.

"Good morning, Paddy," said Kidd cheerfully. "What can I help you with today?"

"Top o' the morning to you, young man," replied Tin-pot Paddy. "I'm in need of a little assistance with my elbow. It squeaks when I do this." He waved his arm in the air to

prove his point.

"I see," said Kidd. "And do you need to do that?"

"What do you mean?"

"Is there any need for you to wave your arm like that?"

Tin-pot Paddy considered this question for a moment. "There's not, now you mention it."

"Then I have fixed your arm, even though I am but an ever-so-humble cabin boy." Kidd bowed.

"Excellent work, Master Kidd." Captain Clockheart patted him on the back, sending him staggering across the deck.

"Och, lad, you're a breath of fresh air around here," said Gadge, sending a burst of stinking steam from his rear.

Kidd wafted away the smelly gas. "Talking of fresh air, I think I might go for a swim, if that's all right with you," he said.

"We have a perfectly good rowing boat if you wish to go ashore," said Captain Clockheart.

"I'm not going ashore. I swim for fun – it's relaxing."

"Not for us it wouldn't be, laddie. I'd sink like a stone as soon as I hit the surface," said Gadge.

"Mr Richmond Swift, our creator, did not have a seafaring life in mind for us," said Lexi.

"Then why did he make you?" Kidd asked.

"We were designed as servants for the king," said Lexi.

"Aye, but we ran away," added Gadge.

"I'll bet he didn't like that one little bit," said Kidd.

"Four thousand little bits, actually." Captain Clockheart strode over to the main mast, which had the latest "Wanted" poster nailed to it. He tore it off and handed it to Kidd.

Kidd whistled, clearly impressed. "A four-thousand pound reward. That's a lot of money."

Captain Clockheart smiled proudly. "Aye, and we're worth every penny. Now, if you're going for a swim, you'd better get on with it. That old rascal Inkybeard will be back soon and then it'll be time to chase this monster."

"Aye aye, Captain." Kidd jumped up on to the barrier and stood on his tiptoes. As he dived he performed a fancy mid-air somersault for the amusement of the crew, who applauded, cheered and sang along to Blower's tune:

We are the Steampunk Pirates,
Despair, despair, despair,
A monster took our treasure,
To its underwater lair,
Kidd's got a plan to find it,
And take the gold what's there,
This cabin boy, In our employ,
Is quick and smart and fair,
(And fair!)
He's quick and smart and fair!

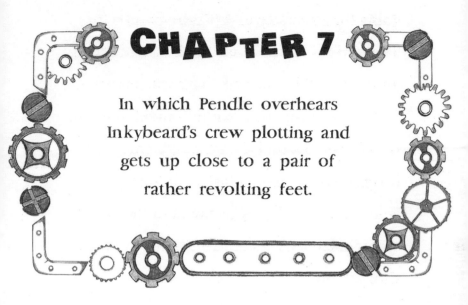

CHAPTER 7

In which Pendle overhears
Inkybeard's crew plotting and
gets up close to a pair of
rather revolting feet.

Pendle hadn't spotted a single friendly
face among Inkybeard's crew since she
had boarded. They were an ugly bunch of
charmless thugs who mostly spoke in low,
grunting voices. When she tried to listen in on
what they were talking about, they fell silent
and stared at her until she walked away.

Since the pirates didn't introduce themselves, Pendle invented her own names for them, such as Scar Face, Broken Nose and Stinky Breath. When the pirate in the crow's nest spotted a merchant ship, it was Stinky Breath who led the attack.

The battle was brief and brutal and, by the time they were finished, the merchant ship was in a terrible state, with its sails torn, masts snapped and half of its crew splashing about in the water. As soon as the looted goods were secured in the hold, the navigator plotted a course for Rotten Apple Harbour, just as they had planned.

Pendle spent most of her time tucked away in the corner of the sleeping quarters, fiddling with her latest clockwork invention, which looked like a small silver egg.

She used a pair of tweezers to make a couple of adjustments, then split the egg in two, listening to every tick and click, as a doctor might listen to a patient's heartbeat.[3] She placed one half of the egg on her hammock and walked to the far end of the dorm with the other. As she moved further away, the ticking slowed down and an arrow on top twizzled around.

"It works," she whispered. "It actually works."

Hearing approaching voices, Pendle grabbed the other half of the egg and took cover under a nearby hammock. Two pairs of feet entered – one with huge purple bunions, the other with extremely hairy toes.

---

3 Impatient readers keen to know what this device does can turn to page 90. But be warned, if you do so, you will miss some very exciting stuff on pages 81–86.

"What's that ticking sound?" said Bunions.

Pendle connected the two halves of the egg and the ticking stopped.

"I can't hear no ticking," replied Hairy Toes. "So are we going to take control of the ship yet?"

"Soon enough," said Bunions. "Soon enough."

Hairy Toes sat on the hammock above Pendle. "Let's do it now."

"No, not yet! We're supposed to wait until we reach Rotten Apple Harbour."

"Why?" Hairy Toes reached down and scratched his right foot, sending flaky bits of skin fluttering to the floor.

"Because it's part of the plan," said Bunions.

"Whose plan? It's not my plan." Hairy Toes scratched his left foot. Several small insects scuttled out and disappeared into the cracks in the floorboards.

"It's Master Kidd's plan. He said Inkybeard will set fire to the ship as soon as he hears the word mutiny. That's why we'll be feeding him to the monster before he gets the chance."

"Oh yeah, right." Hairy Toes chuckled. "Good one." He picked out a lump of dried

meat from between his toes.

"You know that's disgusting, don't you?" said Bunions.

"It's only a bit of breakfast from this morning," said Hairy Toes. "Whoops."

The piece of meat slipped through his fat fingers and landed on the ground.

"You're not still going to eat that, are you?" Bunions asked.

"Waste not, want not." Hairy Toes reached to pick it up but his fingers connected with Pendle. He closed his hand around Pendle's wrist. "What have we here then?" He dragged her out from under the hammock.

"Been spying, have you, lad?" said Bunions. "About to run off and tell Inkybeard what you heard, were you?"

"Er, I... No..."

"Let's see how much spying you can do
from the inside of a barrel!"

Pendle struggled, punched and kicked,
but the men were much stronger than her.
She didn't stand a chance.

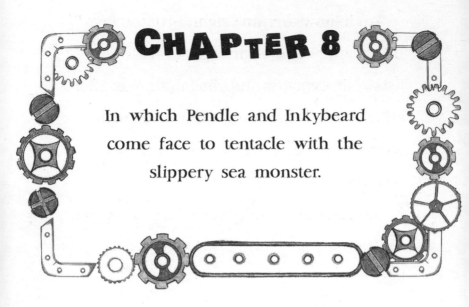

CHAPTER 8

In which Pendle and Inkybeard
come face to tentacle with the
slippery sea monster.

Pendle's cries for help went unheard or
ignored and finally she gave up trying and
sat in the barrel waiting for something to
happen. Eventually she heard the rattle of
the anchor being lowered, the shouts of the
angry crew and the protests of Inkybeard as
he was thrown into the cabin with her.

"Argh, now this ain't right, is it, my love?" Inkybeard pounded on the door with his fists. "My own crew turning mutinous, after all we've done for them. Oh well, time to warm ourselves up with a nice little fire, wouldn't you say, Nell?"

"Inkybeard!" Pendle banged on the barrel.

"Who's that?" said Inkybeard. "Who's in here?"

"It's me ... Pendle. I'm in the barrel!"

"Ah, taking a kip in a barrel, eh? Lovely. Old Inkybeard has spent many a pleasant afternoon snoozing in a barrel."

"I didn't climb in here on purpose."

"Oh, in that case you'll need a hand." Inkybeard prised off the lid and Pendle climbed out. In the centre of the cabin she saw a large wooden chest.

"Thank you," she said.

"Our pleasure. Now, where did old Inkybeard put that match?" He patted down his pockets.

"Inkybeard, look where we are! That's the treasure we stole for bait. They're going to feed us to the monster."

"Nonsense. This crew may be a vile bunch of villainous vipers but... Hold on, what was that noise?"

The octopus tightened its grip on his head, as they heard what sounded like wood being cut.

"Easy now, Nell," said Inkybeard.

They looked over to where the noise was coming from and saw a circular hole appearing. A small spinning blade was cutting the wood.

"It be the slippery sea monster come to take its treasure." Inkybeard ran to the door and rattled the handle. "Come on, lads! Fair's fair," he yelled desperately. "Let us out now."

But the crew was noisily celebrating a successful mutiny and couldn't hear him.

Pendle was unable to tear her eyes away from the hole being cut in the side of the ship. As she watched, a circle of wood the size of a tabletop dropped out. Through the hole in the ship, she could see that the spinning blade was attached to a long silvery tentacle that glinted in the sunlight.

A second tentacle entered the cabin. This one didn't have a spinning blade, but was feeling its way around the side of the room – almost as though it was trying to find something.

While Inkybeard continued to pound his fists on the door, Pendle walked calmly over to the hole and looked down at the ocean. Bubbles rose up, but the rest of the monster was hidden beneath the waves.

"This creature will devour us all," exclaimed Inkybeard.

"Inkybeard, stop panicking. There's more to this than meets the eye," Pendle said, noticing her own reflection in one of the monster's scales. She quickly grabbed a candlestick from the stolen treasure and used it to tap the tentacle.

TINK! TINK! TINK!

"How interesting," she said. "I think it's made of metal."

Pendle turned round and looked on in horror as the second tentacle grabbed Inkybeard's boot.

"Get off me, you beast," he protested, as the tentacle wrapped itself around his leg. Inkybeard whacked it with his cutlass but the creature tugged and dragged him off his feet.

"Nell, if this is your mother again…"

Inkybeard clawed at the floorboards as the tentacle dragged him along the cabin floor and out through the hole, suspending him upside down over the ocean. Below him, the water swirled and foamed.

"Nell, save yourself! It looks like this be the end of the road for old Inkybeard. We only hope we're remembered – perhaps in a song, a poem … or as a beloved character in an exciting children's book."

Whether or not the octopus understood, Nell didn't do as she was told. She clung on to Inkybeard's head.

"The sea monster's creating a whirlpool!" said Pendle. "Inkybeard, don't panic. It's going to drag you straight down. I think you'll be all right."

"Being sucked into a monster's mouth don't sound all right to old Inkybeard."

"Here, catch this." Pendle pulled out the clockwork egg device, snapped it in two and threw one half to Inkybeard.

He grabbed hold of it. "What is it?"

"It will help us locate you."

"We fail to see what use that'll be if we've been eaten by a sea monster."

"Whatever is about to eat you, it's no monster."

"No monster? Then what is it?"

Before Pendle could answer, the tentacle released Inkybeard, dropping him into the whirlpool. Inkybeard vanished from sight in an instant, followed by the tentacles.

Pendle stared down at the bubbles coming up from the submerged monster.

"Time for a spot of monster hunting then?" said a gruff voice as a shadow fell over Pendle. She looked up through the hole in the side of Inkybeard's ship to see Captain Clockheart standing on the deck of the *Leaky Battery*.

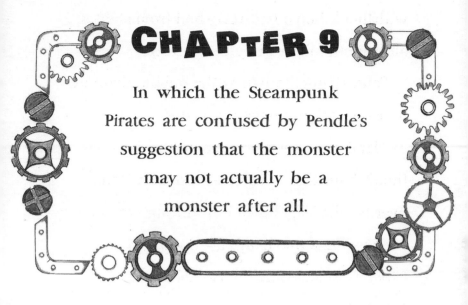

CHAPTER 9

In which the Steampunk
Pirates are confused by Pendle's
suggestion that the monster
may not actually be a
monster after all.

Gadge fired a grappling hook at the hole in
the side of Inkybeard's ship so that Pendle
could climb across. Inkybeard's mutinous
crew threw sponges, buckets and mop
handles, trying to knock her off the rope, but
she moved quickly and was soon safely back
on the *Leaky Battery*.

"They've taken our cabin boy," yelled Scar Face.

"Who cares?" said Broken Nose. "We've still got our treasure."

"I say we capture the Steampunk Pirates and collect that reward," shouted Stinky Breath.

"You'll have to catch us first!" replied Gadge. "And that might be a problem with a hole in your hull." Gadge steered the *Leaky Battery* away, leaving the other ship stranded until the repairs were done.

"Welcome back, Pendle," said Captain Clockheart. "Poor old Inkybeard, eh? Eaten by a sea monster."

"That was no monster," said Pendle.

"Not a monster?" said Gadge. "But it's got tentacles! And didn't you see the bubbles it

was making. What more proof do you want?"

"The tentacle that grabbed Inkybeard was made of metal, and the bubbles are more likely produced by an underwater ship – probably using some kind of steam-powered propeller system."

"An underwater ship?" Lexi's word-wheel turned and clicked. "I can find no record of anything of the sort."

"Maybe young Master Kidd has heard of one," said Gadge.

"Yes, where is he?" asked Pendle. "I've got a feeling he's more involved in this than he's letting on. He told the crew to feed Inkybeard to the monster."

"I've not seen him since he went for that swim," said Lexi.

"Yo ho, down below!" cried Blower. "We've lost the monster's trail. It's too fast for us."

"Oh well," said Lexi. "That's that then."

"Steampunk Pirates don't give up so easily," said Captain Clockheart.

"Exactly," said Pendle. She pulled out the other half of the silver egg.

"Eggs for breakfast!" said Twitter. "Eggs for breakfast!"

"It's not a real egg," said Pendle.

"Then what is it, lad?" asked Captain Clockheart.

"This is a long-range magnetic tracking device that will help us catch whatever – or whoever – took Inkybeard."[4]

---

4 Impatient readers who just turned to this page are advised to go back and continue reading the story from where you left off.

Captain Clockheart inspected it and held it up to his ear. "It's ticking."

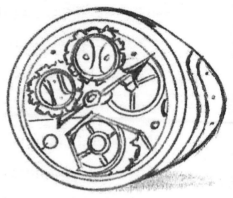

"Yes. Inkybeard has the other half. The closer it gets, the faster this ticks. And that compass there shows us the direction we need to travel."

Captain Clockheart nodded thoughtfully. "I see," he said. "Yes. So how does it work?"

"Er … I just told you."

"Don't worry, I understand," said Lexi. "Now the monster has Inkybeard, we can use this device to follow them, even when they're out of sight."

"Exactly," said Pendle. "Except it's not a monster."

"Hold on." Captain Clockheart scratched his head. "You're saying that the monster is not a monster and this egg is not an egg."

"That's right," said Pendle. "And I strongly suspect that Kidd the cabin boy is not a cabin boy."

"So am I still me?" asked Captain Clockheart.

"Of course."

"That's a relief."

"What about the lair?" said Gadge. "Is that real?"

"All the treasure must be stashed somewhere," said Pendle.

"So you mean we can still get our loot back?" said Captain Clockheart. "Ah, then I say let us use this egg that's not an egg to follow this monster that's not a monster to

find the cabin boy who's not a cabin boy
and get the gold ... which had better be gold
or it'll have me to answer to!"

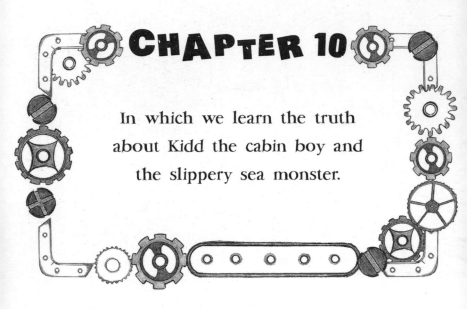

CHAPTER 10

In which we learn the truth
about Kidd the cabin boy and
the slippery sea monster.

The inside of the monster was not as
Inkybeard had imagined. There were dials,
buttons and levers. There were leather seats
and portholes around a dome-like cockpit.

Kidd was sitting back with his feet up on
the control panel. Gas lamps hung in front
of two round windows with tinted red glass.

"The Dread Captain Inkybeard. How kind of you to drop in," Kidd said with a smile.

"Easy now, Nell." Inkybeard patted his octopus. "It's not the end of our story yet."

"Your end will come soon enough," said Kidd.

"But what are you doing here, Master Kidd? What is the meaning of this? Where are we?"

Kidd chuckled. "We are presently four leagues down and travelling deeper, at a rate of five knots. This is a steam-powered, pressurized underwater vessel with the appearance of a sea monster on the outside but all the comforts of a ship on the inside. It's quite a prank, wouldn't you agree? To think, all those pirate ships robbed by me, the ever-so-humble Captain Kidd."

"We're having trouble following you, ain't we, girl?" Inkybeard looked up at Nell. She moved her tentacles in what looked like a shrug.

"I can see that you would like a lengthy explanation and, indeed, mine is a story filled with much drama and many twists. Please, have a seat."

Inkybeard sat down in front of a porthole

and noticed a huge shark swimming alongside the craft.

"Worry not," said Kidd. "The glass makes everything outside seem bigger. It's an illusion, just like the slippery sea monster itself. I'm good at stories, you see. Shall I tell you mine? It begins like this. My name is Charles Kidd. I was born into wealth and sent to the finest school in England, where I proved to be a first-rate student. I would probably have become a great Prime Minister, a renowned scientist or an esteemed author. Tragically, though, tragedy struck. My father was travelling from America to England, carrying with him his entire fortune, when his ship was attacked by pirates. They robbed me of my father and my family fortune."

"Pirates," sighed Inkybeard. "What can you do?"

"I was forced to leave school and take a job on a merchant ship, but that too was attacked."

"Pirates again?" said Inkybeard with a knowing nod.

"Yes. It was then that I realized the only way to recover my father's fortune and to succeed in this world would be to become a pirate myself. Except I would do things differently. I wouldn't steal from the innocent and the honest. I would take only from pirates."

"A pirate who steals from pirates. We knew we liked your style, didn't we, Nell?"

The octopus on Inkybeard's head blinked.

"I won't bore you with the details of how I

made such an impressive underwater craft," continued Kidd.

"But why did you become a cabin boy if you have such a ship?" Inkybeard asked.

"All this time that I've been robbing ships, I have been scouring the oceans for the villain who sunk my father's ship and took my fortune."

Inkybeard adjusted one of Nell's tentacles nervously. "How you getting on with that then?"

"It took me many months to piece together the facts, but I eventually learned that the raid on my father's ship was the first appearance of a pirate with an inky black beard and a sea creature on his head. Now, tell me, do you know anyone who fits that description?"

"Ah, I see," said Inkybeard. "And may I ask why you've been hunting this pirate?"

"Revenge, of course," replied Kidd, with a winning smile. "Revenge."

The author apologizes for this interruption, but he is worried that you may have forgotten about First Mate Mainspring.

The Steampunk Pirates were in pursuit of the sea monster, but First Mate Mainspring had finally achieved his personal ambition of becoming captain of something. Unfortunately for him, he was captain of a small island with nothing more than a tree, a rock, some sand and a number of fallen

coconuts. None of these inhabitants was able to help Mainspring wind up his key. He was hot and his clockwork was running extremely slowly. As a consequence, his mind was playing tricks on him.

"**Cuh-cuh-cuh-click**, now, Mr Tree, this is not going to work out.

Tuh-tuh-tuh-tick, if I'm the … only one putting any effort in. **Tuh-tuh-tuh-tock**, you're too lazy. That's your problem."

"What do you expect? He is a tree," said a fallen coconut.

"**Cuh-cuh-cuh-click**, you keep out of it, Mr Coconut."

"How dare you? Mr, indeed. I'm Mrs

Coconut. Mr Coconut is my husband. He's over there talking to Father Rock."

"**Tuh-tuh-tuh-tick**, stop talking. **Tuh-tuh-tuh-tock**, you're not real."

"Not real?" exclaimed the coconut. "Who are you to turn up here and start saying who is and isn't real?"

"**Cuh-cuh-cuh-click**, well, you're not, are you? **Tuh-tuh-tuh-tick**, I'm imagining you. **Tuh-tuh-tuh-tock**, you're in my mind."

"Who's to say you're not in my mind?"

"**Cuh-cuh-cuh-click**, don't be silly."

"You're the one talking to a coconut."

"**Tuh-tuh-tuh-tick**, you don't exist."

"So you come here and suddenly we exist. But if you weren't around, then we probably wouldn't even make a sound when we hit the ground."

"**Tuh-tuh-tuh-tock**, what?"

"Well, Mr The-only-one-who-exists, I've been doing some calculations," said the coconut pointedly.

Mainspring wondered what kind of calculations a coconut was capable of doing.

"I've worked out that you will be completely wound down within the hour."

"**Cuh-click**, within the hour?"

"That's right." The coconut looked about as smug as a coconut is capable of looking. "Then you'll just be a lifeless lump of metal on a deserted island. This is all your fault, always mutinying and arguing. You even tried to mutiny against Mr Tree here and he's just a tree."

"That was a bit rude," said the tree.

Mainspring turned to look at the tree.

"**Tuh-tick**, you mean you can talk, too?" he said.

"Of course not. I'm a tree," said the tree.

Mainspring knew he was imagining the voices, but that didn't make the coconut's words any less true. Whether or not he was accused falsely, there was no doubt that he had brought this upon himself with his greed and ambition. As this fact sunk in, a single droplet of oil fell from Mr Mainspring's eye.

"You're crying? Pathetic," said the coconut. "What would your Grandfather Clock say if he could see you now?"

"**Tuh-tuh-tuh-tock**, he would say that there is still time and there is still hope," replied Mainspring.

Mainspring was struggling to tell what was

real, so he had no idea if the tree really did make a clicking sound then tip all the way over so that its leaves dipped in the ocean, revealing a large hole in the ground. A jet of water shot from the hole, creating a brief rainbow as it showered down into the ocean.

Mainspring gazed at this beautiful vision in wonder, then he lost his balance and tumbled into the hole. A few moments later, the tree sprang back into place, sealing the hole and leaving Mainspring down at the bottom of the shaft, badly dented and almost completely wound down.

Unfortunately we'll never know if Mainspring made a sound as he crashed to the bottom of the shaft, since there was no one there to hear. Now, let's get on with the story.

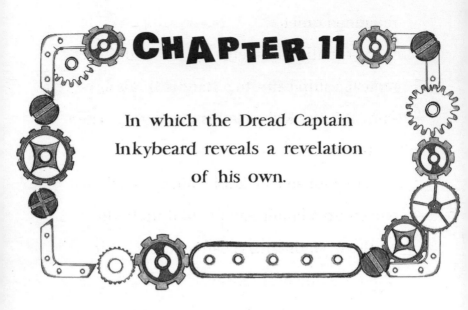

CHAPTER 11

In which the Dread Captain
Inkybeard reveals a revelation
of his own.

Kidd's monster-ship plunged deeper and
deeper, until Inkybeard felt his ears pop and
the blue sparkle of the sunlit water gave way
to blackness.

All the while, Kidd talked and talked
about how brilliant he was to have tracked
down Inkybeard. For his part, Inkybeard

remained quiet.

Eventually the engine cut out and the monster-ship came to a standstill. Then he said, "Master Kidd, Nell is wondering where we be now."

"The monster's lair, of course." Kidd picked up a lantern and held it up to the porthole, so that Inkybeard could see the water outside draining away.

He gasped. "What wizardry is this?"

"This is not wizardry. It's Whizz-Kidd-ry." Kidd chuckled. "The water is being drained away from the outer cave using a series of pumping air vents that lead to the surface."

Inkybeard felt a shudder as the ship settled on the rocky bottom of the underwater cave.

"Now, would you be so kind as to open

the hatch behind you?" Kidd picked up a pistol and pointed it at Inkybeard.

"Open a hatch in a ship on the belly of the ocean?" said Inkybeard. "Are you madder than me?"

"Worry not. I designed this all myself," said Kidd. "Now, the door, please." Kidd waggled the pistol at him.

Inkybeard opened the hatch cautiously and then stepped out.

Kidd followed him with a lamp. Its flickering light filled the cave, allowing Inkybeard to see the outside of the remarkable underwater ship. "Hey, what do you know? It does look like your mother, Nell."

Nell squeezed his head.

"Easy now, girl," he said. "It was only a joke."

"There's another hatch behind you," said Kidd. "Go through it."

Inkybeard did as he was told. Kidd lit another lamp, revealing a second cave, bigger than the first and rammed full of treasure. Kidd followed Inkybeard inside.

Inkybeard gasped. "Argh, now this be an impressive haul, to be sure! But why are we here?"

"To make a deposit."

"But you collected no treasure from my ship – just me and Nell."

Kidd stood in the doorway, his eyes sparkling. "You are my treasure. You were the pirate who robbed me of my fortune."

"And now you intend to share yours with me. Is that it?" Inkybeard chuckled. "That's very generous of you, lad."

"In a way. You will remain in this cave until I come back and decide what to do with you. However, there is no food or water down here and no way out. By the time I return, you'll be a pile of bones. Goodbye, Captain Inkybeard. Goodbye, Nell."

Kidd turned to leave.

"It just so happens that we remember your father's ship," said Inkybeard.

"You do?" Kidd stopped in the doorway.

"Aye, I remember it well. Only you're wrong. Inkybeard never robbed it. The truth is that your old man lost his money before setting sail for England."

"What are you blathering about?"

"Yes, he lost his money in a dubious investment in the Americas.[5] But as he crossed the ocean, an idea occurred to him to

_____

5 Those of you who have read *The Leaky Battery Sets Sail* will be interested to know that the name of the man behind this investment was Chas Goldman. Those of you who haven't read this excellent novel should do so at once!

make money another way. He would become a pirate. He took control of the ship, then grew a long, thick beard as black as ink."

"What are you saying?" said Kidd, raising the pistol once more.

"Old Inkybeard didn't sink your father, Kidd," said Inkybeard. "Old Inkybeard *is* your father."

Kidd paused in the doorway and, for a moment, the glint in his eyes dimmed. "Dad?"

"Barney Kidd, at your service." Inkybeard offered his hand. "We knew it the moment we met you, but we couldn't find a way to tell you. You're our son, Kidd. You're our boy." Inkybeard threw his arms open. "Son."

Kidd's eyes blackened with anger. "In which case, you deserve this even more." He slammed the door shut, leaving Inkybeard and Nell in the gloomy cave.

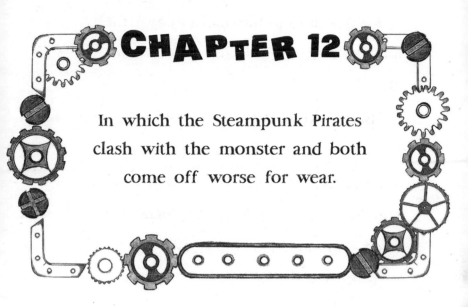

CHAPTER 12

In which the Steampunk Pirates
clash with the monster and both
come off worse for wear.

No matter how many times Pendle tried to
explain how the tracking device worked,
no one except Lexi could understand her.
The *Leaky Battery* had been travelling in the
direction of the compass arrow for hours
when Gadge finally said, "The ticking on
your egg is speeding up, laddie."

"That means we're gaining on the monster." Pendle surveyed the horizon. "We should be able to see it by now."

"Yo ho, island ahead!" yelled Blower.

"I say, isn't that where we left Mainspring?" asked Lexi.

"That be the island, indeed." Captain Clockheart grabbed a telescope from his belt. "But I see no sign of our first mate."

"Never mind old clickerty-tick-tock. What about this monster?" said Gadge. "Pendle, are you sure this egg of yours actually—"

CRUNCH!

The *Leaky Battery* suddenly tilted to the left, sending its crew staggering to the side. Loose barrels and buckets rolled straight over the edge of the ship. One of them

knocked Mr Pumps clean off his feet. He would have fallen had Loose-screw not grabbed hold of his bandana and kept him on board.

On the lower deck, the cannons hit the side of the ship with such force that they crashed through the wood and dropped into the ocean.

"What's happening?" asked Lexi.

A pair of twisting tentacles appeared on deck. One of them coiled itself around the main mast, while another sliced into the side of the ship with a spinning blade.

"It's the monster," yelled Rust-knuckles.

Captain Clockheart tried to slice through a tentacle with his cutlass, but another appeared and clamped around his wrist. More wrapped themselves around his legs.

"A bit of assistance would be most welcome," said Captain Clockheart.

"Right you are, Captain." Gadge switched to a rifle attachment and fired at the tentacles. They retreated, releasing Captain Clockheart.

Pendle peered over the side of the ship and saw more tentacles cutting into the

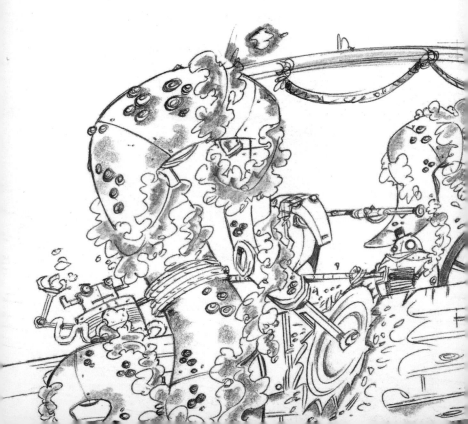

ship's hull. "It's trying to sink us!"

"Water in the hold," came a cry from below.

"Bail her out," yelled Captain Clockheart. "Mr Gadge, we need to get that hull repaired and we need it repaired now."

"Aye aye, Captain." But Gadge was having difficulty climbing up the deck, with the ship at such an angle.

"We're all going to die!" squawked Twitter, flapping above their heads. "We're all going to die!"

"Not if I have a plan to save us, we won't," said Captain Clockheart.

"Well? Do you have a plan to save us?" asked Lexi, who was clinging on to the mast with both hands.

"Of course I do," said Captain Clockheart, "My plan is that one of us needs to come up with a plan. Now, who's got a plan?"

"That's not a plan," said Pendle.

"I'm afraid Twitter's right," said Lexi. "We are all going to die."

"We need to fire at Kidd's ship," said Pendle. "An underwater ship like that will be pressurized. It will only take one direct

hit to bring it up."

"Och, now that I can do." Gadge selected his cannon attachment, reached his arm over the side of the ship and fired a mini-cannonball into the water.

Suddenly, the *Leaky Battery* rocked back into an upright position, flinging the crew over to the other side of the ship.

"Up she rises," said Captain Clockheart.

A huge metal ship in the shape of an octopus emerged from the water. Its tentacles had released the *Leaky Battery* and were thrashing about in the water, as the monster-ship tried to stay afloat.

Gadge's cannonball had smashed the glass in one of the monster's eyes, revealing Kidd inside. He was soaking wet and looking distinctly unhappy.

"Look what you've done to my monster-ship," he cried.

"Sorry about that, Master Kidd!" said Captain Clockheart.

"Just as I thought," said Pendle. "This monster contraption was an invention of yours."

"Contraption?" exclaimed Kidd. "This is a far finer example of steam engineering than your floating tin cans." He opened a hatch in the top of his ship and climbed out.

"Och, at least we are floating, laddie," said Gadge.

"Whereas you appear to be sinking," added Lexi.

Kidd clung on desperately as his monster-ship filled with water. "There's no chance I could catch a lift with you,

I suppose?" he asked.

"Catch a lift?" exclaimed Pendle. "If you had your way, we'd be at the bottom of the ocean right now."

"Yo ho, down below! Ship ahoy!" called Blower.

"If that's Inkybeard's crew, we'll teach them what's what," said Captain Clockheart.

Pendle looked around at the damage caused by Kidd's attack. "We're in no position to fight anyone," she said.

"Wait a minute!" said Gadge, switching to his telescopic-eye attachment. "That's no jolly roger. The ship's flying the union jack."

"Oh dear," said Lexi. "It's the king's navy and with our ship half torn apart and our cannons sunk, we're sitting ducks."

"Ha, I wouldn't want to be in your boat."

Kidd chuckled. "I say, that's rather funny. And when I tell the commander of this navy ship how I am the one who put you in this position, he'll probably give me a medal. Oh, I say, things are looking up for the ever-so-humble cabin boy," said Kidd.

"Not funny! Not funny!" squawked Twitter.

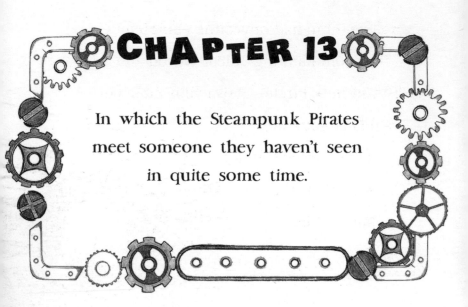

CHAPTER 13

In which the Steampunk Pirates meet someone they haven't seen in quite some time.

The navy warship slowed down as it approached. All along the deck, red-coated soldiers stood with muskets and rifles aimed at the Steampunk Pirates. Rows of cannons stuck out from the side of the ship.

The pirates grabbed what weapons they could find, while Kidd trod water. His

monster-ship had now sunk completely.

The commanding officer waved and cried, "Steampunk Pirates. Raise your hands or we'll sink your ship."

"Never," cried Captain Clockheart, as the ship lurched suddenly to the side. One of the crossbeams snapped and banged him on the head.

"Captain," said Pendle. "We're letting in water. We have no cannons to defend ourselves. One hit and we'll be sunk."

"The Steampunk Pirates don't admit defeat," said Captain Clockheart. "It's not in our nature."

"Good men of the navy," yelled Kidd from

the water. "I am on your side. 'Twas I who did this damage to the *Leaky Battery*."

The commanding officer was about to reply when another voice came from below deck. "Corporal Thudchump, is it safe to come up?"

"The pirates are refusing to surrender, but they have a badly damaged ship. There's also a swimming boy. I was about to open fire on all of them."

"Hold on. I would like a word with my servants first."

A small man with a fur-lined coat and a golden crown on his head stepped out on deck.

"All hail, His Majesty, the King of England," cried Corporal Thudchump, saluting.

The soldiers raised their guns and saluted.

"Ah, there you are, my Steampunk
Servants," said the king. "You lot have
caused me quite enough trouble. Quite
enough, indeed. I say, why is there a boy
in the water?"

"Your Majesty," said Kidd, swimming
towards the ship. "Mine is the story of a
boy who was badly wronged by pirates,
and yet—"

"Silence. You'll show more respect and

bow before royalty," the king said.

"Yes, Your Majesty." Kidd bowed, but as he was swimming, this meant that he disappeared under the water.

The king turned to address Captain Clockheart. "You there, with the clock on your chest, would I be right in thinking you are in charge?"

"Aye," replied Captain Clockheart. "I be the captain of this ship."

"Then you simply must give the command to surrender. Do so at once and I will take you back. I'll have Mr Swift turn you into obedient servants again. It is your only chance of survival."

"Unfortunately, I think he's right about that," said Pendle.

"I agree," said Lexi. "If we fight we'll be

defeated ... sunk ... obliterated."

"Och, I hate to admit it, but we've got no choice," said Gadge.

"That's where you're all wrong," said Captain Clockheart. "There is always a choice. I may not always choose the wisest course of action. Nor the safest. But if you ask me to choose between being a slave and roaming free, Steampunk Pirates will always take freedom."

"We're all going to die!" squawked Twitter.

"Your Majesty," yelled Kidd. "I will happily surrender. As an ever-so-humble cabin boy, my story is one with—"

"Someone get that boy on board," said the king.

"Thank you, Your Majesty," said Kidd.

"And gag his mouth to stop him talking."

"And what of the Steampunk Pirates?" asked Corporal Thudchump.

"If they won't surrender, sink their ship and be done with them."

"Cannon-bearers, musketeers and riflers, prepare to fire," commanded Corporal Thudchump.

"Our chances of survival are too small to calculate," said Lexi. "They are miniscule … tiny … teeny weeny."

"I think I can hear the approach of the ghost train." Captain Clockheart solemnly raised his fist. "All hail the Steampunk Pirates!"

"So this is it then," said Pendle. "This is how our adventures end."

"Och, and if that's not bad enough, I think it's raining," said Gadge.

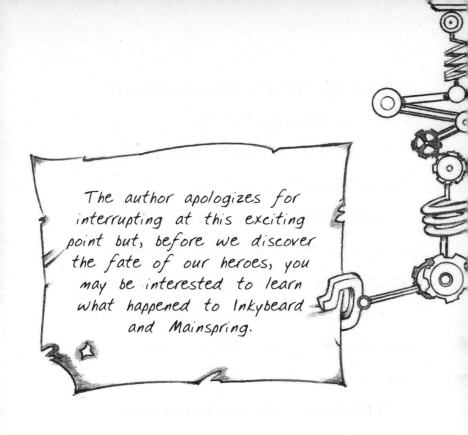

The author apologizes for interrupting at this exciting point but, before we discover the fate of our heroes, you may be interested to learn what happened to Inkybeard and Mainspring.

Inkybeard was stuck in a cave, surrounded by huge mounds of gold, buckets of rubies and mountains of diamonds. He sat down on a pile of precious silk underwear and picked up an emerald the size of his fist.

"Nell girl," he sighed. "We be in a right pickle this time."

"**Cuh-cuh-cuh-click** ... **wuh-wuh-wuh**-wind
... me **uh-uh-uh**-up."

"Who's down here?" Inkybeard jumped
up and spun round to see who had spoken.

"**Tuh-tuh-tuh-tick**..."

The voice belonged to a mechanical man
with a large key in his back, lying on his side.

Inkybeard sat him upright. "Inkybeard
recognizes this heap of junk. You're
one of the Steampunk Pirates!" He gave
Mainspring's key a couple of turns and
heard the whirring, clicking and ticking of
him coming to life.

"**Tock**, thank you."

"So are you one of the machines with useful devices to get us out of here?" said Inkybeard.

"**Click**, no, I'm the scheming one. **Tick**, and I have a scheme to get us out of this hole. **Tock**, all I need is something to light a fire."

"Then you're in luck." Inkybeard patted his pockets then reached inside his right boot and pulled out a match. "I knew I'd put it somewhere safe. So, what's this plan of yours?"

"**Click**, we take gunpowder from our pistols, then blow a hole in the side of the cave."

"A hole? There's nothing but ocean on the other side of these walls."

"**Tick**, exactly. The water will come

rushing in. We'll each get inside a trunk positioned under one of these shafts that lead up to the surface. **Tock**, the force of the water will push us up the shaft and we'll be free."

"Blow a hole in the side of a cave many leagues below sea level, flood the cave with several gallons of ocean water and lock ourselves in trunks? This be madness," said Inkybeard. "Luckily, old Inkybeard embraces madness as other sailors embrace scurvy and warts. Let's do it."

Now, if you are sitting comfortably, it is time for the final chapter of this enthralling adventure.

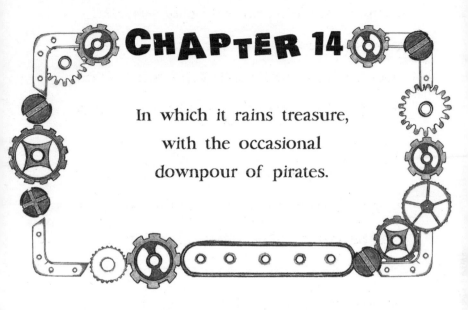

CHAPTER 14

In which it rains treasure,
with the occasional
downpour of pirates.

Things had never looked worse for the
Steampunk Pirates. A hundred guns had
been loaded and every single one was
pointing their way. Their ship was unarmed
and letting in water. Kidd was safely on
the navy ship, managing to look smug even
though his mouth had been gagged.

"Yo ho, goodbye to all I know," yelled Blower, with a final whistle.

"It has been an honour serving with you all," said Captain Clockheart. "Rust-knuckles, Washer Williams, Mr Pumps—"

"Ow." Something heavy hit Pendle on the head.

"I'll thank you not to interrupt, Pendle lad," said Captain Clockheart. "I'm making a final speech."

"Sorry, Captain. It's just that something hit me." She bent down to pick it up, but Captain Clockheart grabbed it first. It was a coin. He tested it between his teeth before announcing, "Gold. It be raining gold!" He looked up and another coin hit him in the eye.

"Pennies from heaven! Pennies from heaven!" Twitter swooped and swerved to

avoid being hit, as more coins came down.

The soldiers on the navy ship dived for cover, but the tough, metal-bodied pirates were unaffected by the shower of coins.

Captain Clockheart snatched a glistening jewel from the sky. "Look at this. There's jewels, too. This be a downpour of treasure."

"How is that possible?" asked Pendle.

Twitter was turning figure of eights and loop the loops to avoid getting hit. "What goes up!" he squawked. "Must come down!"

"Look," said Pendle. "It's all coming from the island."

In the middle of the island was what looked like an erupting volcano of treasure.

Small pieces were followed by heavier ones, then two large wooden trunks flew into the air.

One landed in the sea next to the island, while the other knocked the mast head off the navy ship and splashed down between the two ships.

"Corporal Thudchump, don't just stand there," yelled the king. "Get us out of here. These raining coins are tearing our ship apart!"

"Turn the ship about," cried Thudchump.

"What on earth is going on?" asked Lexi.

A lid popped open on the nearest chest and Mainspring appeared. "**Click**, oh, you lot are back, are you? **Tick**, come to apologize, have you? **Tock**, well, I don't forgive you for leaving me."

"Then I won't waste my time on apologies," said Captain Clockheart. "Instead, I'll ask whether you would like to remain captain of that wooden chest or return to your role as first mate of this pirate ship."

"**Click**, oh, very well," Mainspring replied.

"Drop the rope ladder," said Gadge. "Let's get him up."

By the time Mainspring had climbed on board, the last of the treasure had fallen and the king's ship was sailing away as fast as it could manage.

"**Tick**, who was that?" asked Mainsping.

"No one important," replied Captain Clockheart.

"In actual fact," said Lexi, "the King of England is one of the most important people in the world."

"Not to me, he's not," said Captain Clockheart. "The only important people are right here on this leaky old vessel." He picked up a coin and tossed it into the air.

Twitter swooped down and caught it in his beak. "Or just above it!" he said, dropping the coin to the deck.

"Captain, this ship is still badly in need of repair," said Gadge.

"Aye, and I know I can trust you to get this crew working on it straight away."

"But what happened to Inkybeard?" asked Pendle.

"Over here," yelled a voice from the island.

Inkybeard was sitting on the beach with an open chest beside him. Nell was clinging on to his head tighter than ever, obviously

alarmed by the ordeal she had just been through. "You wouldn't leave a fellow pirate stranded here!"

"Don't you know?" said Gadge. "There's no such thing as a fellow pirate."

"Very true, Mr Gadge. Goodbye, Inkybeard," said Captain Clockheart. "Until next time."

"**Tock**, goodbye, Mr Tree," Mainspring waved at the island.

"Are you feeling all right, First Mate Mainspring?" asked Lexi.

"**Click**, never better. **Tick**, you see, down in that cave I had more treasure than I'd ever dreamed of. **Tock**, but what use was that without my freedom?"

"Now, there is a lesson for you, Pendle," said Captain Clockheart. "I know how you

like to find morals in our adventures."

"That's not the moral of this," said Pendle. "Kidd betrayed us and tried to sink us just as Inkybeard and all those others we've met have done. The moral is that we should not trust anyone."

"That's not right," said Gadge. "We met you, didn't we? Remember? Back in the king's kitchen when you showed us our true path. That day we put our trust in you."

"That's very true, Mr Gadge," said Captain Clockheart, "but we're Steampunk Pirates. We're not here to learn lessons. We're here to fight and loot and claim our reward. We're here to seek bright horizons and to make our future rich with golden opportunities. Now, my badly bolted buccaneers, let's get this ship shipshape. Gadge, a song is required."

"Aye aye, Captain."

As the Steampunk Pirates set about repairing the damaged ship, Gadge threw his head back and sang:

We are the Steampunk Pirates,
We'll never strike a deal,
We're made from iron and copper,
And a few small bits of steel,
We fought a slippery monster,
It tried to tip our keel,
But in its lid,
Was a lad called Kidd,
No, that monster wasn't real,
(Not real!)
The monster wasn't real!

READ THEM ALL!

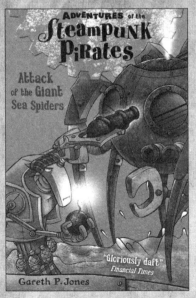

eBooks available

CHAPTER 1

In which our heroes,
the Steampunk Pirates, attack the
HMS Regency, and its commander,
Admiral Fussington, demonstrates
how, when it comes to surrendering,
the English are second to none.

At first glance, there was nothing especially remarkable about the pirate ship that emerged from the thick sea mist and drew alongside the *HMS Regency*. Its billowing sails were white. Its flapping flag was black. Its crew of ragged buccaneers jeered and cheered and waved their razor-sharp cutlasses as their captain cried, "Surrender, you English mummy's boys or we'll fire up the cannons and blast more holes in your ship than you'll find in a barrel full of Dutch cheese, so we will."

However, these were no ordinary pirates. Under the captain's dark blue hat was a face made of metal that glinted in the sunlight. Steam shot out of his ears and his head. He wore a heavy woollen coat, open at the front to reveal a clock on his chest. It had only one hand that was madly whizzing around.

"Oh no, it's the *Leaky Battery*!" cried the terrified lookout on the *HMS Regency*. "It's Captain Clockheart and the Steampunk Pirates!"

Captain Clockheart laughed. "You hear

that, First Mate Mainspring? Load up the cannons."

"**Click**, aye. **Tick**, aye. **Tock**, Captain," replied a pirate with a bowler hat, chequered trousers and a large key slowly rotating in the middle of his back.

"We surrender!" Admiral Fussington immediately raised his hands.

"Load 'em up and prepare to… Hold on. Did you say *surrender*?"

"Yes! Don't fire – we give up." Admiral Fussington turned to his crew. "Sergeant Thudchump, order your soldiers to lower their weapons."

The sergeant motioned to the rest of the crew and they reluctantly put down their guns.

The hand on the captain's clock suddenly

stopped and steam *put-put-putted* out of his head in confusion. "I don't understand."

"Och. Let's blast 'em to smithereens. Surrendering is no way to stop us attacking," snarled Mr Gadge, who wore a tartan kilt and bandana to match, and had a hook in place of his left hand. He twisted his arm and the hook was replaced with a cannon ramrod.

"Hold your fire, Gadge," said the captain. "I'd like to know why a ship of the Royal Navy would surrender so quickly."

A mechanical bird with a few colourful feathers glued to its wings landed on his shoulder and squawked, "A bunch of scaredy cats!"

"How rude. Not at all," protested Admiral Fussington. "I'm simply following the latest guidelines with regards to P.C.S.s."

"Ah, ignore Twitter," said Captain Clockheart. "What's a P.C.S. when it's at home?"

"A potential conflict situation. The rules now state that senior officers should immediately surrender. Look, I've got a kit and everything." The admiral opened a bag and pulled out a stick with a white flag wrapped around it. After carefully reading the instructions, he unfurled the flag and gave it a little wave.

Captain Clockheart laughed then turned to the rest of his crew, who joined in, their mechanical jaws clanking and clinking.

"Right, you lot," yelled the captain. "First Mate Mainspring, lower the boarding planks. Gadge, Loose-screw, Blind Bob

Bolt and the rest of you merciless metallic marauders ... PREPARE TO BOARD!"

Gadge fired a grappling hook at the neighbouring ship's main sail and all the pirates cheered. All except for one, who wore a frilly shirt and had a device at the top of his head, which sent small bits of paper flitting around, making a fluttering sound as they turned.

"Ahem, if I may have a word, sir."

"What is it, Quartermaster Lexi?" snapped Captain Clockheart, the vapour from his head twisting up like a mini-tornado.

"I'm not sure that boarding this vessel is altogether a good idea," he replied anxiously.

"Spoil sport! Spoil sport!" squawked Twitter.

"Quite right," said Captain Clockheart.

"That's not fair," protested Lexi. "I'm just

saying that the chances of this being—"

Captain Clockheart banged the back of Lexi's head and the quartermaster instantly went quiet and stopped moving. "That's better. There's a good reason why the only one of us with any brains has an off switch." He laughed. "Piracy's not about thinking or worrying – it's about taking what you can!"

The captain's clock hand began to move quickly again and he cried, "Now, you horrible lot, all aboard this ship before I send you to the sharks for dillying and dallying. Take all the gold and coal you can find."

The crew of the *Leaky Battery* lowered the boarding planks and made their way over to the *HMS Regency*, where the smartly dressed naval officers stood with their raised hands shaking in fear.

"Search the ship," ordered Captain Clockheart.

"Yes. Take whatever you need," said Admiral Fussington, who was still waving his white flag.

"I like this new policy of yours, Admiral," said Captain Clockheart. "Now, would you be so kind as to empty your pockets and hand over your … GOLD." The steam shot excitedly from the pirate's nostrils as he said the word.

The admiral pulled out a small purse. "This is all the money I have," he said.

Captain Clockheart emptied the coins into his palm and tested one between his metal teeth.

"Do you … eat metal?" asked the admiral, looking equally intrigued and appalled.

"Eat it?" said Captain Clockheart, with a low chuckle. "No, we don't eat it. The fire in our bellies requires coal and wood."

"Then what do you want with it?"

"Let me show you." Captain Clockheart pulled back his sleeve to reveal that his wrist was made of gold. "I saved up my booty from the last three raids to make this beauty."

"Why would you want gold body parts?"

"Because our maker saw fit to craft us from iron, a metal that rusts. The salt water eats away at our parts something horrible. And there's nothing more painful than rusty nuts and bolts, I can tell you. We don't wear these rags for comfort, warmth or modesty. We need to protect our metal from the elements, so we do."

"But there are other metals that don't rust…" the admiral pointed out. "Copper or silver are easier to find than gold."

"Ah, but nothing *feels* like gold," said Captain Clockheart. "A soft-skinned landlubber like you wouldn't understand. Gold is the finest of all metals and, one day, I'll have more than a gold wrist. One day, this entire ship will glisten with golden glory. Then maybe we'll give up this pirating lark for good. But until then … hand over your booty."

"Gloriously daft"
Financial Times

"A rollercoaster ride"
Armadillo Magazine

"A really great adventure"
Darcey, age 7
Lovereading4kids reviewer

"Full of zany humour, piratical
puns and oceanic action"
Parents in Touch

"A winning mash-up"
The Telegraph

"Brilliant"
Tomasz, age 9
Lovereading4kids reviewer

Gareth P. Jones is the author of
many books for children, including the
Ninja Meerkats series, *Constable & Toop*
and *The Considine Curse* (winner of the
Blue Peter Book of the Year 2012).

When he isn't writing, Gareth can be found
messing about in south-east London with
his wife, Lisa, and their children, Herbie
and Autumn. He spends an awful lot of time
turning himself into a Steampunk Pirate. He
has made a beard out of springs, a detachable
clock heart and is currently learning how to
play sea shanties on an accordion.

Find out more at:
www.garethwrites.co.uk